I'm Swift Heart Rabbit. Remember that no matter how busy life gets, there's always time to spread happiness and good cheer.

I'm Proud Heart Cat, and I want you to remember that you should take pride in yourself and do your best in everything you attempt.

My job is to remind you that loyalty and honesty are the things upon which you build true friendship. That's why my name is Loyal Heart Dog.

Making others feel confident and comfortable is the most important job I can think of. That's why I'm known as Cozy Heart Penguin.

I'm Treat Heart Pig, and I say that any day can be a holiday when you help others enjoy themselves.

Now that you've met all of the Care Bear Cousins, we hope that you'll want to become our friends just as much as we want to be friends with you.

Care Bears, Care Bear Cousins, Tenderheart Bear, Friend Bear, Grumpy Bear, Birthday Bear, Cheer Bear, Funshine Bear, Love-a-Lot Bear, Wish Bear, Good Luck Bear, Brave Heart Lion, Gentle Heart Lamb, Swift Heart Rabbit, Bright Heart Raccoon, Lotsa Heart Elephant, Playful Heart Monkey, Proud Heart Cat, Cozy Heart Penguin, Treat Heart Pig, Loyal Heart Dog are trademarks of American Greetings Corporation.

Library of Congress Cataloging in Publication Data: Plummer, Louise. A walk to grow on. (A Tale from the Care Bear Cousins) SUMMARY: When Jennifer has trouble with her job walking pets, the Care Bear Cousins help her learn that solutions come from not giving up. 1. Children's stories, American.
[1. Perseverance (Ethics) — Fiction. 2. Occupations — Fiction. 3. Animals — Fiction]
I. Title. II. Series.
PZ7.P734Wal 1985 [E] 85-505 ISBN 0-910313-85-7
Manufactured in the United States of America 1 2 3 4 5 6 7 8 9 0 -01

PROOF OF PURCHASE
A Walk to Grow On.
C.B.C.

Care Bear
COUSINS

A Walk to Grow On

Story by Louise Plummer
Pictures by Tom Cooke

Everyone in Jennifer's house had a job except Jennifer, who was the youngest. Jennifer wanted a grown-up job, too. Then maybe she would be grown-up just like everyone else in the family seemed to be.

So one morning Jennifer announced in a bold voice, "I am going to get a job!"

"You're crazy," said her brother. "You're too young."

Her mother reached out and took Jennifer's hand. "Jennifer, honey," she asked, "Why do you want a job? Do you need more money?"

Jennifer tried to explain. "I'm the youngest in the family. I'm the only one who doesn't have a job. I want a job, too."

"You can make my bed," said her sister.

"No thank you," said Jennifer. "I am going to find a real grown-up job that I can do all by myself." She left the table and went outside.

When she sat outside on the front steps,
however, she could not think of where to
look for a job. It was going to be hard trying
to be a grown-up person.

Then a sudden breeze caught the edge of
the morning paper that lay at Jennifer's feet,
and it blew open.

She started to close the paper when she noticed a picture of a boy walking a dog. Jennifer stared at the picture. Suddenly she got the *best* idea! "That's it!" she said. "That could be my job. I can walk pets for my job!"

"I knew you'd get the idea if you just
stopped to read. Reading can give you lots of
ideas," said a bright and friendly voice.

Jennifer looked around to see where
the voice had come from. There, standing
by the corner of the house, was a raccoon
with a heart that looked like a light bulb on
its tummy.

"Who are you?" Jennifer asked. "Was that
you talking?"

"Of course it was," said the raccoon. "Don't you know me? I'm Bright Heart Raccoon, one of the Care Bear Cousins."

"Care Bear Cousins? I've heard of the Care Bears, but not…"

"Oh, you'll soon find out about us," Bright Heart Raccoon interrupted. "We're very much like the Care Bears, but we believe in acting on the way you feel. 'Go out there and do something about it,' is what we say."

"Are all the Cousins raccoons?" Jennifer asked.

Bright Heart gave a little laugh and said, "Oh, no. We're all kinds of animals."

"Can I meet you all?" asked Jennifer.

"I don't think you'll have to," replied Bright Heart. "You see, we only leave the Forest of Feelings, the place where we live, when we know that a boy or girl needs one of us especially. Now I knew that you needed a bright idea, so I thought I'd help you find one."

"Thanks," said Jennifer.

"Don't thank me yet," said Bright Heart. "In my book an idea isn't much good unless you do something about it. Now that you've thought of walking pets, what are you going to *do* about it?"

Jennifer bit her lip and thought. Then she rushed inside to get some crayons and stiff paper. She was going to tell everyone about her idea. She lay down and began to print.

Later that afternoon, Jennifer stood on
the street corner. She waited…and she
waited some more. No one seemed to be out
walking. No one stopped to read her sign.
Jennifer began to get discouraged. Then
a big, black car drew up next to the curb.
A woman rolled down the back window of
the car and said, "Hello, Jennifer. What a
good idea you have. My usual dog-sitter is
on vacation. Can you walk my Fifi around
the block for the next few days?"

"Hi, Mrs. Palmer," Jennifer said. Mrs. Palmer lived in the big house around the corner. "I'd love to walk Fifi," Jennifer continued.

"Good," said Mrs. Palmer. "Do come by early, won't you, dear?"

Jennifer nodded. Mrs. Palmer rolled up the window of the big, black car, and off she went.

The mailman walked by. He said, "Do
you think you can handle a *big* dog?"

"Yes, sir," said Jennifer.

"Then come by my house on Green Street
tomorrow morning, and you can take Goliath
for a walk," the mailman said.

Jennifer watched the mailman walk down the street. "Now I will have one whole dollar from my job," she thought proudly.

"Hey, Jennifer, you really want a job?"

Jennifer looked around and saw Sally, a girl in her class.

"Yes, I do," said Jennifer.

"Good. I have to go visit my grandmother, and she doesn't like dogs. Come by tomorrow morning. Tasha, my dog, will be waiting."

"Gee, thanks, Sally," said Jennifer.

Next, Jennifer was hired by a man who said he had an unusual pet that needed walking, and finally by a woman who said that her pet, Lily, was sensitive.

As she walked home thinking about the money she was going to make, Jennifer was joined by Bright Heart.

"I'm so glad you got those jobs," Bright Heart said. "You didn't take too many, did you? Five is a great many pets."

"Don't worry," Jennifer said, "I can manage them all."

The next morning Jennifer woke up before the alarm went off. She could hardly wait for her new job to begin. She quickly dressed, ate, and left the house.

The butler answered the door at Mrs. Palmer's house. He stared down at Jennifer. "Be careful with Fifi," he said. "She is a very valuable dog."

"I'll be careful," Jennifer answered.

She walked to the mailman's house with Fifi scampering beside her. When the mailman opened the door, Jennifer found herself staring into the eyes of a dog that was as big as she was.

"Meet Goliath," the mailman said. "Don't worry, he's very gentle."

"I hope so," said Jennifer.

Jennifer started down the street toward
Tasha's house. Goliath pulled at the leash.
She and Fifi hurried along.

Sally brought Tasha out. "I just shampooed
and brushed her," Sally said. "Try to keep
her clean." Jennifer nodded, and with
Goliath leading, they all trotted quickly to
the next house.

"This is Mr. Bob. Don't worry. He doesn't spray anymore," said Mr. Bob's owner.

Jennifer stared. "It's not a dog," she blurted. "It's a skunk!"

"You promised you'd walk him," said the man. He closed the door. Goliath barked at Mr. Bob. Fifi yapped.

"Shhh," said Jennifer. "It's early. You'll wake everyone up." She still had one more pet to pick up. When she got to the house, she left the other pets tied to a tree in the front yard and rang the bell. When Jennifer saw the last pet, she said, "Oh, no!"

Lily, a Persian cat, was sensitive and shy. She wanted to walk behind Jennifer or between her feet. Lily definitely did not want to walk with the dogs and the skunk.

Jennifer stumbled along for a while. The dogs barked, the cat yowled. The skunk looked worried.

Then Lily's leash caught around Jennifer's leg. She stumbled and fell. The leashes pulled free from her hand, and all the pets ran away.

"Come back! Come back!" yelled Jennifer, but the pets did not listen to her.

Jennifer was very discouraged. How would she ever get the pets back together again? As she was thinking, something flashed by her and came to a stop a few feet away. Jennifer blinked her eyes. It was a rabbit, and it had a heart with wings on its tummy.

"Hello, hello," the rabbit said very quickly. "I've come to help."

"Are you one of the Care Bear Cousins?" Jennifer asked.

"Of course, of course. I'm Swift Heart Rabbit, and it looks like you need my help."

"I need somebody's help," Jennifer answered.

"Then, here's what to do. Get up and run quickly just like I do. Catch Goliath first since he's the quickest. Then get the rest. Don't just sit there. The pets will really get away if you don't act quickly. Understand? Fine! Good Luck!" and as quickly as he had appeared, the rabbit was gone.

Jennifer thought about what Swift Heart Rabbit had said. It certainly was true that nothing good was likely to happen if she just sat around, so she quickly ran after Goliath.

After a little while, she had rounded up all the pets. "Those Care Bear Cousins really have been helpful," she thought, "but I hope they don't have to help me again today."

Unfortunately, just at that moment, Goliath and Fifi both saw a squirrel scampering across the grass. With a bark and a yap, the two dogs ran toward the squirrel.

"Whoa! Whoa!" called Jennifer, holding on tight as she and the other pets were pulled across the lawn.

Splash!

Jennifer and all the pets went into a big mud puddle. Lily, the Persian cat, yowled. Fifi yapped. Tasha's shampooed coat was filthy. Goliath now seemed to have lost all interest in the squirrel, and he stood in the middle of the puddle taking a big drink.

Jennifer had never felt worse in her life. Still holding the leashes, she sat down on the ground. A small tear trickled down her cheek. The pets seemed to understand her mood, and they gathered around and looked at her with worry in their eyes.

"Jennifer," a soft, deep voice said. "Please stop crying. Let's try to figure out how you can feel better."

Jennifer looked around. The voice came from another Care Bear Cousin, an elephant, and on its tummy was a weight with hearts on it.

"My goodness," said Jennifer, drying her eyes. "What's your name?"

"Lotsa Heart is my name," answered the elephant. "I like to help well-meaning children like you."

"I don't think that you can help me. I guess I was too young to get a job."

"Nonsense," replied Lotsa Heart. "Walking pets is a fine job for you. You just didn't realize how many pets it was possible to walk at once. That's what you learn if you stick to a job, and don't let it get you down. Why, before long you can be the champion pet walker in this whole town."

"Really?" Jennifer asked.

"Really," said Lotsa Heart. "But right now we've got to do something about these dirty, noisy animals. What do you do when you are dirty?"

"I take a bath."

"Hmmm," said Lotsa Heart. "Your house is only half a block away. If you tied half the pets to that fence over there, took half home, and then came back for the others, I bet you could put that hose in your backyard to good use. What do you think?"

Jennifer's eyes lit up. "Thanks, Lotsa Heart. That's a great idea."

"Well, it's not bad, and if you stick to it, you'll have those pets cleaned up in no time."

Jennifer did just what Lotsa Heart had suggested, while Lotsa Heart and the two other Care Bear Cousins watched. She washed and brushed each animal until it was clean and shiny again. Then one by one, she took the pets home to their owners. She earned two dollars and fifty cents. When she looked at the money in her hand, she felt glad.

"I can do a grown-up job," she said, "but next time I'll walk the pets one at a time."

"Good idea," said Lotsa Heart. "Good ideas come to those who never give up."

"And who keep reading," said Bright Heart.

"And who move fast," added Swift Heart.

"Thanks. I've got to go now, but I couldn't have done it without all of you."

"Remember, we'll be keeping an eye on you from our home in the Forest of Feelings," said Lotsa Heart.

The Care Bear Cousins waved good-bye, and Jennifer turned and went into her house. Her family was sitting around the kitchen table. "Hey, Mom," said Jennifer. "What would a grown-up do with two dollars and fifty cents?"

Meet the Care Bear Cousins

They help you put your good feelings into action. The pictures on their tummies tell what's special about each one of this great group.

Hello! I'm Brave Heart Lion; it's my job to show that you can be a leader if you have kindness in your heart.

I'm Playful Heart Monkey. I love good times, and I want to remind you that fun can be found everywhere if you have joy in your heart.

 *(Lotsa Heart Elephant illustration appears at left)*

My name is Lotsa Heart Elephant, and my job is to show you that your real strength shows through when you never say, "it can't be done."

I'm Bright Heart Raccoon, and I want to show you that learning can be fun, especially when the solution to the problem helps a friend.

I'm here to show you that when someone is in need, the best cure is love and kindness. That's why they call me Gentle Heart Lamb.